EARLY BIRD
STORIES

The Four Little Pigs

Early ★ Reader

First American edition published in 2019 by Lerner Publishing Group, Inc.

An original concept by Kimara Nye
Copyright © 2020 Kimara Nye

Illustrated by Marcin Bruchnalski

First published by Maverick Arts Publishing Limited

Maverick
arts publishing

Licensed Edition
The Four Little Pigs

Lerner Publications Company
A division of Lerner Publishing Group, Inc.
241 First Avenue North
Minneapolis, MN 55401 USA

For reading levels and more information, look up this title at
www.lernerbooks.com.

Main body text set in Mikado. Typeface provided by HVD Fonts.

Library of Congress Cataloging-in-Publication Data

Names: Nye, Kimara, author. | Bruchnalski, Marcin, illustrator.
Title: The four little pigs / by Kimara Nye ; illustrated by Marcin Bruchnalski.
Description: Minneapolis : Lerner Publications, [2019] | Series: Early bird readers.
    Purple (Early bird stories) | "The original picture book text for this story has
    been modified by the author to be an early reader." | Originally published in
    Horsham, West Sussex by Maverick Arts Publishing Ltd. in 2016.
Identifiers: LCCN 2018043868 (print) | LCCN 2018052766 (ebook) |
    ISBN 9781541561809 (eb pdf) | ISBN 9781541542273 (lb : alk. paper)
Subjects: LCSH: Readers (Primary) | Characters and characteristics in
    literature—Juvenile literature. | Swine—Juvenile literature. | Witches—
    Juvenile literature.
Classification: LCC PE1119 (ebook) | LCC PE1119 .N94 2019 (print) |
    DDC 428.6/2—dc23

LC record available at https://lccn.loc.gov/2018043868

Manufactured in the United States of America
1-45401-39035-10/19/2018

EARLY BIRD
STORIES

The Four
Little Pigs

Kimara Nye

Illustrated by
Marcin Bruchnalski

Lerner Publications ◆ Minneapolis

Tom's Granny Mag is a bit unusual . . .
she's a witch!

Whenever Tom stays with her, something
magical always happens.

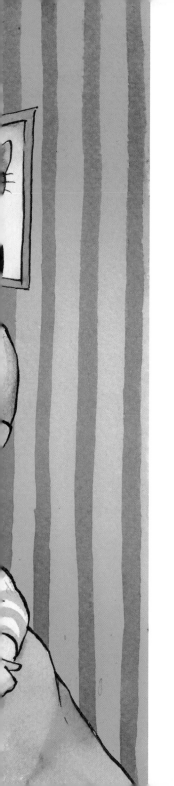

One night, Granny Mag read Tom
a bedtime story.

"Once there were three little pigs,"
she began.

"I know that story!" said Tom.
"It's boring."

The Three
Little Pigs

Granny Mag smiled. "Let's make it more exciting," she said.

"Abracadabra! With this spell,

You'll enter the tale you know so well!"

Tom landed beside three houses—one
made of straw, one made of sticks, and
one made of bricks.

"I'm a pig!" Tom thought. "I'm in the story!

I must warn the three little pigs about the wolf!"

The pig in the straw house was making tea.

"The wolf is coming!" Tom cried.

"Don't worry," said the pig.

"He can't get into my house."

Suddenly, someone banged on the door.

"Little pig, little pig, LET ME IN,"

the wolf shouted.

"No way!" replied the little pig.

"Then I'll huff, and I'll puff, and I'll blow

your house in!" roared the wolf. He breathed

in . . . just as Tom threw some pepper at him.

AAAACCCCCHHHOOOO!

"Fine," the wolf spluttered. "I'll get your brothers instead!"

"Let's warn my brothers!" cried the little pig, and they ran from the house.

But the pig in the wood house didn't believe them.

"The wolf can't blow my house down," he said.

"Oh yes he can, but don't worry," said Tom,

"I've got a plan!"

The wolf decided to try being polite.

He knocked gently on the door of

the wood house and stepped inside.

But Tom had put soap on the floor!

The wolf slipped across the room.

WHOOSH!

Tom and the little pigs ran to the

brick house.

The wolf followed them.

"LET ME IN!" he howled.

"Or what?" Tom asked. "You'll blow the house in?"

"Hey! That's my line," said the wolf.

He huffed and puffed, but he couldn't blow the house down.

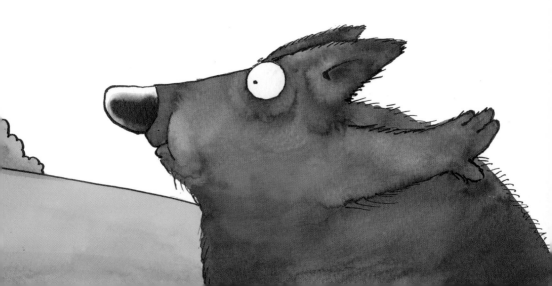

The four little pigs were happy—until

they heard footsteps on the roof.

"Oh no!" cried Tom. "The chimney!"

The wolf crashed down the chimney.

"I'm not afraid of bullies like you!"

Tom shouted.

The wolf looked fed up.

"I'm hungry and tired," he said. "I'm

going to Little Red Riding Hood's

house—she makes

great cookies."

As the wolf ran away, Tom turned to the little pigs.

"Now you can live happily ever after!"

He felt Granny Mag's magic swirl around him . . .

The next moment, Tom was back in bed.

"So, was that boring?" asked Granny Mag.

"No!" said Tom. "Let's read *Little Red Riding Hood* tomorrow. I hear her cookies are great!"

Tom looked down at the book.

Something had changed . . .

"I love having a witch for a grandma," said Tom.

"Goodnight, Granny Mag!"

Quiz

1. What is the name of the story that Granny Mag reads to Tom?
   a) *Little Red Riding Hood*
   b) *Jack and the Beanstalk*
   c) *The Three Little Pigs*

2. What does Tom throw to make the wolf sneeze?
   a) Dust
   b) Pepper
   c) Flour

3. What is the third house made of?
   a) Sticks
   b) Straw
   c) Bricks

4. How does the wolf get into the third house?

   a) He goes down the chimney.

   b) He climbs through a window.

   c) He knocks politely.

5. Why does the wolf want to go to Red Riding Hood's house?

   a) She makes great cookies.

   b) He wants to dress up as her grandma.

   c) He thinks she'll taste nice.

COLOR		GRL
Purple	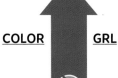	J-K
Orange		H-J
Green		G-I
Blue		E-G
Yellow		C-E
Red		C-D
Pink		A-C

Leveled for Guided Reading

Early Bird Stories have been edited and leveled by leading educational consultants to correspond with guided reading levels. The levels are assigned by taking into account the content, language style, layout, and phonics used in each book.

As Quiet as a MOUSE

Cookie Blast Off!

The Dessert That Wouldn't Wobble

The First Underwear

The Four Little Pigs

The Great Grizzly Race

Grumpy King Colin

Hocus Pocus Diplodocus

Preposterous Rhinoceros

A Royal Mess